Shikarı Babu's of Odisha

(based on the life of
B.S. Ray)

Sreemoyee Das

First Published in July 2021

ISBN: 978-93-5427-845-7

BLUEROSE PUBLISHERS
www.bluerosepublishers.com
info@bluerosepublishers.com
+91 8882 898 898

Cover Design:
Palak

Typographic Design:
Namrata Saini

Distributed by: BlueRose, Amazon, Flipkart, Shopclues

DEDICATION

To my father, Late Mr. Samar Singha Ray

ACKNOWLEDGEMENTS

My uncle, Mr. Bir Singha Ray, who is the narrator of this book. Most of the stories are based on his real life experiences. Without his blessings and able guidance, this book wouldn't have been possible.

My Husband, Sanchit Das, for being my pillar of strength and my Pole star.

My son, Shaurya Veer Das, whose warm embrace and cherubic face, keeps me going.

My mother, Sabita Ray, for always believing in me and also for being my biggest critic.

My Father in law and mother in law, my second parents, Mr. BK Das and Sasmita Das, for their encouragement and blessings.

Zoyi, Zubi and Shikha di for being the fuel to the fire of my life.

My friend and guide, Sucheta Wadkar, what would I do without you?

CONTENTS

NARRATOR'S DECLARATION

About a century back, for that is almost what my age is spiraling to, we could never predict how the tables would turn! Our simple hobbies and nonchalant ways of living brought about mass extinction of precious animals. I still sift through the old photo albums and stare at the younger me, proudly posing with a big game and wonder, 'why'?

I have learnt it the hard way that each life, however tiny or mighty, is equally precious. I have felt the pangs of piercing agony felt by parents when separated from their children, the day when my only son left me mourning in a terrible road accident. It left my wife paralysed and broke something within me permanently. It put me in deep retrospection; never did we stop to think about the motherless cubs while hunting a tigress, we had brought them as gifts back home for the younger ones to play with or presented them to the local kings and the royalty.

Today, I am a changed man, for these old bones have suffered the malevolent twists of fate and these matured eyes have witnessed sweeping tragedies. It took me a while to realise that the viridescent cover is diminishing rapidly. Our wildlife is precious and now precarious, the real beauty of our planet, it needs to be protected right here and now. Although I deem it impossible to reverse the damages we have already inflicted on the earth, any efforts to restore it is extremely crucial today. Balance in nature is what sustains us and that balance is long lost. I urge all my readers to do whatever little they can to nourish this earth back to health. The least that everyone can do is not to repeat the mistakes of the bygone generations. At the final chapters of my life, how I wish I could go back and undo the injuries that we had so casually inflicted on earth. This book, by no means, is meant to glorify the life of hunters.

INTRODUCTION

A long time ago, before the concrete jungles arrested the natural ones, before politicians started running the nation, before the age of air and water purifiers, before families became nuclear and nuclear became bombs and before smiles were made of plastic, there was a time which ran at its own pace. There existed forests and woods all over the Indian subcontinent, so deep and dark, so mystique and haunting, so bewildering and enchanting that even sunlight was not permitted to kiss the ground in places. India as a nation was still verdant and bountiful while its men were more endurant, curious and adventurous. There was more life in the forests than in the cities today. The forests were overpopulated with love and friendship between the most unlikely creatures that you can comprehend. The forest functioned as an organic whole, with its own terms and conditions, its own code of conduct for the residents to follow, its own language and even punishments meted out for not obeying rules. At that time, most villages and even some cities in India were circled by sporadic woods that usually densed into forests. This layout made the confrontation between man and the wild almost customary, frequent and well expected.

It seems just like yesterday when we had enough fish in the streams, fruits on the branches and oxygen in the air to label this world as a welcoming homely place. Today, although I don't venture out much, my idiot box tells me that there are more plastic bags in the ocean than fish, more carbon in our air than in our copier machines and more fruits in our soaps than on our plates. It was not so then, when we were young, we were easily satisfied, say, with a flower blooming in the garden. Many of us were thrill-seekers, really really adventurous, despite our typical bollywood-like mothers trying all sorts of blackmailing techniques to hold our foot from perils.

'What joy lies in routine'? our young blood used to ask. Forests were a constant source of mystery for us as we crossed adolescence. The deep-dark-haunting trails would lure us with whispers and fire our imagination up as children. As we started to grow up, we gathered both courage and information on how to venture into the trails. All forest encounters were not tragic and violent though, each day was full of surprises. Sometimes, a deer may saunter by and try to befriend you while you are gathering wood for the kitchen. The children befriended the rabbits and squirrels, chased them around, often giving them nicknames on regular meetings. Some families who couldn't afford teddy bears for their children, would instead gift them with real bear cubs to play with, like we did. Animals around us ensured lots of joy and laughter, friendship, compassion and of course, a lot of mess!

Then there were reasons to be terrified of the forests, the big games causing chaos and havoc, chasing people out and often destroying life and property. When I speak of my experiences, it mostly comprises my time in Odisha's jungles, for it had become a part of me. I evolved with it, with its familiar smells and sounds, the narrow trails leading me out of the monotonous world into a world of haunting and mysterious fulfillment. The animals and the insects were as familiar to me as the people I grew up with.

The forests are no more in abundance but their memory is still verdant in my mind. Odisha's forests were dotted with bison, wild buffaloes, a variety of deers, bears, wild hares and many more species. Then, there were Tigers, plenty of them turning into man-eaters; intelligent, majestic, swift, hostile and perennially hungry. They spread terror within and outside the limits of the forest, hunting down both man and beast with the same precision. By looking at a tiger no one can guess if it's a man-eater or not but the biggest catch is, you will not live to tell the difference if it were indeed a man-eater. I have heard of Lions being rewarded with the 'King of the Jungles' title but have you ever seen a tiger in the wild? There is nothing more royal and majestic than a tiger simply sauntering by. There is an aura of Lordship they claim simply by the way they conduct themselves, hunting or not. Being a frequent visitor to the forests, I have had the fortune of observing the ways of the wild and to be candid, the wilderness is more disciplined than we humans declare ourselves to be. I have seen animals using frantic sign languages to alert each other when a tiger is on the prowl. There was a certain species of bird, I know not its sophisticated nomenclature but locally we called it the 'Tee-Tee' bird, owing to the shrill sound it made alerting everyone if there was a tiger approaching. Then there were monkeys who would go for an Olympic run and climb up the trees with great speed and make weird faces at each other and chattering loudly. Many times, while waiting for a tiger, I have been alerted of its approach by the messengers of the forest.

If Lions are 'king of the jungles', Tigers are the Gladiators then; skillful, alert, lethal. The forests had two types of tigers; the regular carnivores and the man-eaters. The latter wouldn't hesitate to infringe human territories, take stock of the situation, go back, make a master plan and come back prepared. Some of them hunted human prey with such precision and skill that the person sleeping next to the prey wouldn't be aware of the attack until he woke up the next day.

Lastly, there were 'us', at the top of this whole lethal chain, the hunters or 'shikaris' as referred to locally. There were a lot of variations in this category too. Some hunters were small game chasers, some hunted for food, others for killing time, some hunted for the thrill of it. Indian Kings and Prince's took great pride in their hunting skills and occasionally arranged hunting parades to amuse themselves or a Royal guest. The Britishers, who introduced themselves as mere traders when they first came in and later changed their mind, had a deep intrigue for the Indian forests as well. There were highly skilled professionals appointed to kill man-eaters only, with a promise of reward from the local Rajas or even the British government. These men were real experts, trained or untrained, they eventually mastered the game of tracking and hunting down these extreme predators.

I was a trained but not so skilled shikari who self coached himself largely about the ways of the forest. I had received some valuable guidance from my father and some highly skilled shikaris until I decided to go out into the wild all by myself, to observe and learn. I had quite a few unusual encounters with the forest beasts and have lived long enough to share some of my experiences with my readers.

SHIKARI BABU

Our human nature forces us to imitate our elders, what we see them do, we invariably try to copy as children. My passion for hunting was inspired mostly by the elders of my family, my father being on top of the list. My father, Mr. Satish Chandra Ray, was a true disciplinarian. He had his own book of rules for the forest as well as the family. He was not one of mild temperament and had a very adventurous but short life. A soldier in the Bengal Regiment during the World War 1, an expert in artillery and Literature alike, a true philanthropist, a Travelling-Ticket-Inspector on the Bengal-Nagpur Railways and a timber merchant later on, his multifaceted life took him places and everytime he returned home armed with more knowledge and courage than before.

Once, during his days with the British army, he was sent to Iraq from his regiment to counter the Turkish advances. In a small battle, the British troops advanced deep into the enemy territory and gunned down the Turk forces. However, on their way back, my father and his friend Mr. Ranada Saha, were trapped in the counter attack and taken prisoner by the Turks. After a few days in the prison camp, they were to be transferred to the Turkish jail from Iraq as war prisoners and held there for eternity.

The war camp of the Turks was on the bank of the Tigris river, from where they used to draw water daily on horse drawn tankers. The prisoners, under the vigilant eyes of a rifle-held sentry, were to draw buckets of water from the river and fill the tankers. This job was allotted to my father along with other inmates. After a week of this tiresome filling-refilling business, my father grew desperate, knowing that soon they will be tossed into the Turkish Jail from where there will be no return. He and his friend hatched a rudimentary plot to escape the camp, leaving much for destiny to decide, knowing very well that if found escaping, they will be gunned down mercilessly.

The next morning, they went back to the river and worked patiently till dusk under close vigilance. When the last three horses were about to leave, it was completely dark and the sentry, tired. They took two of the horses near the bank to load the tankers and used their bodies as a shield. As soon as the sentry turned, they took one dip in the Tigris and never surfaced until well away from sight. After swimming underwater for quite some time, they bobbed up their heads to look for signs of danger, but there was none until then. They had calculated that, in the dark, their absence would completely go unnoticed until the next morning. However, they were still in enemy territory and not totally out of danger. Also, walking barefoot could lead to more peril than swimming to safety, they thought. Taking advantage of the darkness, they slowly swam downstream all night. After moving downstream for twelve miles or so they finally took to dry land. Few more miles of walking and enquiring led them to a British camp nearby from where they were rescued.

Post this adventure, when he came back to India, he became the Travelling-Ticket-Inspector for Bengal-Nagpur Railways Co. Later, he quit his job and eventually became a timber merchant and a forest contractor. In his new role, he had unrestricted access to the forest and being his eldest son, I too enjoyed the perks and perils of it. I naturally got absorbed into his timber business and thereby being absorbed into the flora and fauna of Odisha's jungles.

Father was an excellent hunter, someone with mathematical precision, who could aim only at the sound and make a kill. Had he been alive today, I would have surely urged him for the Olympics. But unlike us, he had his own rulebook, which said "guns are not meant for fun" or something like that I believe! He wouldn't kill for recreation, nor would he ever kill an animal when it is feeding or suckling. So accurate were his targets and so comprehensive his knowledge of the forests that the locals lovingly called him "Shikari Babu". He lamented the reckless hunting he had done in his younger days and was almost bound by oath not to kill for pleasure or sport. He would spring into action (in the later years of his life) if and only if there was a threat from some animal or rogue animals, especially tigers. There were several instances when he used to be summoned by the District Magistrate to kill man-eaters in exchange for a reward. Those days there was a fixed rate card for killing rogue animals, chartered by the Sub-Divisional Magistrates (in Odisha). It went like this:

Rs 100 for a tiger

Rs 50 for a bison

Rs 50 for a leopard/panther

Rs 50 for wild boars etc.

Let's not forget that fifty Indian rupees could make any man's fortune then. One had to produce either the entire dead animal or its head to claim the prize money from the

Magistrates office. This practice of giving rewards to murderous hunters may seem appalling now but this was a time when there were more animals in the wild than men in domesticity. So the ratio of men to animals was not so weak then and animals often did more harm to people than vice-versa. However, this practice obviously had a negative impact on wildlife, as more and more hunters started to crowd the forests being lured by the cash reward. This led to more mishappenings, like one amateur hunter killing the other by mistake and so on. I never claimed any reward whatsoever but the practice itself gave way to rampant butchery and also rivalry among hunters.

Being the eldest son of my family, I was chosen to escort my father on his hunting trips as a helper and pupil. He would teach me about the ways and perils of hunting, the risks involved and the ways to counter them. There was a lot to learn from him and simply wandering in the forest with him was an enriching experience. Of course he had his favourite shikari friends and helpers who would follow him even to death. During my forest internship with father and his aides, we had numerous thrilling experiences, some of which I shall narrate shortly.

Father (on the right) with the man-eater.

SHIKARI BABU AND THE MAN EATER

One day when my father had just settled down for a hearty lunch along with some of his cousins, a young peasant came howling right onto our verandah, crying in his native language for help. It took us a good five minutes to calm him down and understand his nasal accent. What we understood was that he was out in the pastures nearby, along with his father to feed the cows. It was raining elephants and rhinos, so they had entered the woods at the fringe of the field, to take cover from rain. The father and son were hiding in the woods, under the shelter of broad leaves to avoid being soaked, leaving the poor cows to fend for themselves. They were unaware of a man-eater on a prowl nearby. Unfortunately, the Royal Bengal tiger chose this poor lad's father as his meal, leaving the cows for a later target. The tiger had been lying in ambush and pounced on them unaware. The distressed lad described how, with a great blow it struck his father to the ground before dragging him away. The father screamed out to his son to run to safety fearing they both would perish. The young man was trembling as he narrated the incident, shocked and disconsolate. His wailing and howling brought more curious villagers to our verandah, who also enquired what's for lunch that day!

My father promptly sprung up, ditching his barely touched rice and mutton curry prepared fondly by my mother. He washed his hands and laid them straight unto his new. 500 bore rifle and loaded it with bullets, meanwhile ordering his helpers to get ready immediately. I had by then, thankfully, savored my delectable meal and wasted no time to join the search party.

We went to the spot in the woods where the lad had described the attack. My father and his helpers thoroughly scrutinised the area for any clues and pug marks to help us trace the tiger quickly. Due to the rain, the damp soil had pug marks etched fresh in its bosom, marks that led deep into the woods, towards the dense forest. We chased the marks for some distance until it got completely concealed in wet leaves and grass. We split into two groups and silently advanced deep into the forest. After about a fifteen minutes walk, we could hear a low trembling voice weeping, "Harey Krishna Harey Rama-Harey Krishna Harey Rama" (Hindu prayer) repeatedly, as if praying to the lord for mercy. We stood there in pin-drop silence, transfixed, alert, while my father tried to gauge the direction of the voice. He then waved his hand to signal us and the four of us tiptoed towards that direction, behind my father. The second party who had split up for the search soon joined us. Other than my father, the search party included me, some of fathers' trained helpers and then there was my fathers favourite aide, Rama. He was a strong, muscular man in his mid forties, once a highway robber, who later swore complete devotion to my father until his death. Rama was an adept archer, extremely skillful with his 'Batul' (local version of the slingshot).

Following the voice carefully, we came upon a clear patch in the forest; the voice was now clear, "Harey Rama Hare Krishna" it mumbled. With my father leading the way, we came by an old fig tree and took cover behind it. Peeping from behind the trunk, we saw them! An unimaginably huge Bengal Tiger, on a tuft of grass. It looked majestic to me; yellow and black striped body, a long tail and an intimidating disposition. Although at this point it looked somewhat not so lethal, panting slowly with its mouth open, lazing on its stomach and looking away from the miserable sight of a middle aged puny man who lay almost parallel to him, trembling and chanting the name of the Almighty but unable to move. Tigers, more often than not, love to play a cruel game of catch and go with their prey, not killing it at one go, but chasing it and hunting it down again and again. The tiger will first tame a prey with a fierce blow and drag it away to some secluded safe spot and if by then the prey is still conscious, it let's the prey go, which sprints away with all it's might but the tiger chases it and captures it again. It repeats this play until both are exhausted and then it finally decides to settle the matter by striking the prey down one final time. We had only heard of this treacherous behaviour of tigers from word of mouth, never witnessed it ourselves. I began to wonder if it did the same with this poor peasant.

The tiger was looking away from its prey, confident that he was in control, while the poor man, oblivious of the help at hand, kept mumbling to God for help, with whatever energy that was left in him. We knew we had to save this man at any cost, since we were there just in time for rescue. We had a large team but there was a tricky situation at hand. If we fired a bullet and by chance it missed the tiger, it would first blow off the poor man's skull, mistaking the sound for some trick played by the prey. However, if we did manage to hit the tiger and the bullet missed it's head and lodged itself in any other part of the tiger's body, then too, the poor man would be killed by a doubly angry wounded tiger, worse still, it could straight come for us. From where we positioned ourselves, we could only aim at the tigers back, for it looked away from us and there was no way to aim between the eyes, which was the only way to keep the man alive. A tigers' sense of hearing is as acute as a dog's, even better I would say, this I can vouch for through a lot of first hand experiences. This meant it was impossible for us to move about and try to change our positions, for our footsteps would invariably alert the tiger. Also, there were too many of us, which would have made us clumsy.

Time was running out and though we were armed, we dared not fire and injure the tiger. We all spoke in sign language as was the norm when in a big group. We left the decision making to my father, who was the most experienced man in the group that day. Any other time, it would be fine to take a second chance but not this time, the peasant's life was in jeopardy. It is believed that an injured tiger is thrice as dangerous as a regular one, so we all tried several permutations and combinations in our minds to make the undertaking a success. Suddenly, without any warning or consultation, my father fired two rounds in the air. We were as taken aback as the tiger at this firing! It got startled and confused and sprung up on all fours like an alarmed domestic cat! It looked at the prey for some clue, but saw him lay motionless, groaning. Without losing much time in investigation, it ran for cover, much to our relief.

All this while, the poor man was unaware of his rescue operation but as soon as the tiger was out of sight, he tried to lift his head up and looked around in confusion. Once we were sure that the tiger was safely out of reach, we hurried to the wounded man's rescue. It was quite a dreadful sight to behold. The flesh from his right shoulder was bitten off and the blood had congealed forming an awful spectacle. He had a deep cut across his face made by the tiger's claws, thankfully sparing both his eyes and had also lost a lot of blood from the injured shoulder. He looked weak and half dead from anxiety and had to be helped to sit upright. We carried him safely back to our home, gave a little first aid and then my father arranged for him to be sent to the Cuttack Medical School (now Medical College). Sadly, he perished in a painful death by the spread of gangrene from the tiger's bite. When the news of his demise came, my father was visibly upset, for all his efforts in the rescue operation went futile. He now decided to go after the tiger before it inflicted any more harm to the villagers.

A few days later, the tiger was spotted again by the locals. For my father, hunting was not a full time hobby nor could he set out whenever he wished to. He had to constantly switch between his Railways job which he then had, to entertaining the unending train of guests that invaded our home all four seasons of the year, to travelling extensively for the business venture that he was planning to undertake. However, this particular tiger became a target for my father and he left no stone unturned to go after it. With the help of the villagers, a trap was set up in the nearby forest. A full grown robust goat was used as bait, hoping that it would work, considering the fact that it found human flesh more tempting, which was impossible to arrange!

My father, along with his companions, set up a 'machan' (a makeshift platform erected on a tall tree, to keep watch during hunting) on a nearby tall tree to keep watch. This was close to a fresh water body, where pugmarks had been noticed only two days ago. I was not permitted on this mission unfortunately and had to make do only with the second hand account of what ensued.

It was decided, that my father was to stay on the 'machan' all night, keeping alert for any signs of the tiger, while his companions, who were chosen by the magistrate himself (it included an amateur hunter and an even more amateur torch bearer), were to lodge on another machan on a tree opposite to that of my fathers' and be equally vigilant. So they did wait patiently all night while the anguished goat bleated it's heart out drawing all sorts of curious guests to the spot. A bison nonchalantly passed by followed by three deers who sauntered around the goat and went away, even a bear came up to answer the distressed goat but the tiger never came. Having had a long and tiresome day, my father dozed off on the machan and he woke up next to curse the forest insects for disturbing his sleep, only to realise it was the break of dawn. The mosquitoes and bugs make for irritating music when you are trying to sleep. The forest has its own music too, that gets especially eerie at night. Any first timer camping in the forest at night might as well have a heart attack from being startled by such music. It has the rustling of leaves in the dark by unknown sources, weird mating calls by treeborne birds and animals. Some birds call out like they are warning you of an impending death, while the crickets rub themselves crazy, creating a sonorous chirping. My father, of course, was quite familiar with the spooky ambience of the forest nights and could even differentiate between the sounds. All thanks to his numerous night expeditions that had trained his ears to the jungle jingles. Shortly after my father woke up from his slumber, he heard a distinct sound which he was almost waiting for. At dawn, the tiger had come to the water-hole for an early morning drink. When a tiger laps up water with its tongue, it makes a subtle "clik clik" sound, which is quite distinct from the other sounds in the forest. My father sprung up on his machan knowing that the tiger was at hand. He signalled his companions to stay alert too, although those two looked no better than the sleepy goat below. From the tree on which my father was perched, he had a partial view of the water-hole, so he came down and took cover behind another robust tree trunk, from where he could clearly mark the tiger. The tiger lapped up water for some time and then lifted it's head up just to ensure that there was no danger around and then continued it's drink. After a hearty drink, it settled down on a tuft of grass and began to roll on it. The goat was still bleating in intervals, very weakly now as it was exhausted after screaming the whole night. All night, it's bleating had brought about many enquiring animals who sniffed and went, perhaps even sympathised. This tiger, however, was not interested. A successful man-eater's ego perhaps! It paid no heed to the bleating and carried on playing with the grass.

All this while, my father waited patiently, watching this deadly, yet marvellous creature amusing itself like a little kitten. He later told us that he didn't want to kill any animal while it was eating or drinking and waited long after it settled down. My father left his hiding spot and sneaked up near a fallen dead tree from where he could aim at the man-eater. He signalled the others to remain on the machan, for any confusion or noise would immediately alert the tiger.

The beast of a bullet that my father fired, was meant for elephant hunting and there was no way the tiger could have survived the shot. The bullet lodged itself in the tiger's neck, making it spring up in surprise and then it fell with a thud on the grass. It tried to get up and run but in vain. In about three minutes, life gave up on it and it lay motionless on the ground. The hunting party waited for over a good half an hour before venturing anywhere near it. It's a thumb rule to first use various ways to see if the tiger is responding or not. Some choose to throw a small stone near it, or poke it with a stick from as far as possible, if it is alive, one would come to know. In this case, a long bamboo stick was used by the other hunter to poke the tigers back to see if it responded but the tiger was long gone. On close inspection, they saw that the bullet had hit the windpipe, killing the tiger quite fast. It took a good two hours labour and four men to tie the tiger up and carry it to the truck.

When they came home, I was out on the porch, eagerly awaiting their arrival along with the other family members. The tiger was brought in first, a royal looking one and really huge it was, although not the biggest one I had seen but definitely worth the chills. Almost the whole neighbourhood broke into our house within fifteen minutes to have a look at the fallen "devil", as they used to call man-eaters then. My father and the others returned to their charpoy and settled themselves with pride and composure, letting the youngsters behave like hooligans while they sipped hot tea.

SHIKARI BABU AND THE ROGUE ELEPHANT

Father adored elephants, and so do I. The colossal gentle beasts of the forest are a marvel to witness. With their cute calves and their mammoth tusks, they can surely melt your heart. In his wildest dreams, my father would have never imagined to have a perilous encounter with them. Destiny, of course, as always, has other plans!

It was October, and like most Indian families, we too were busy with festivities, immersed in frolic, the house full to the brim with guests and laughter, the kitchen aromas often attracting uninvited guests. Cousins and uncles swarmed the courtyard and the garden, while the ladies giggled and hushed each other up. My mother who could easily surpass all degrees in cursing sometimes, too was in a jovial mood. There was one big, unending party going on in our house when a man barged in with news of a prowling man-eater nearby.

All hell broke loose! I do not know what it was with my father and man-eaters; as if there was some invisible motor inside him that kick-started involuntarily and dragged him to his guns at the news of man-eaters. He never reacted similarly to other tigers that were not human tasters! He put an immediate halt to all our Tomfoolery and went in to put on his olive green shirt and boots. Olive green coloured shirts were a huntsman's best friend in our times, the camouflage attires were not yet so popular. The colour seamlessly blended with the lushness of the forest and barely made one visible with a little skill. Sometimes we used to draw three black stripes on our faces to make ourselves even more indistinguishable from the surroundings. My father occasionally wore boots, my favourites in the forest however, were light canvas shoes, produced even then by the 'Bata' company. There were two varieties of it, now popularly called Keds, white ones used for tennis and sports and muddy-earth-red ones used for various other purposes. Boots are more protective in the forest, but it is not a good option while chasing a prey, especially tigers, for they creak and make even more messy sounds during the rains. While in the forest, on a hunting mission, it is very important to be as quiet as possible, for most animals have an acute sense of hearing and creaking boots can give your location away. I also preferred to go barefoot, especially when chasing prey in the woods and paddy fields. It gives you immense agility and balance, it's also the most soundproof method. It has its own risks though, for more than once I had almost three inches of thorns pierced into my foot and suffered terribly agony for weeks, that's a story for later.

My father commanded me to join in the hunt but this time I reluctantly joined them, complaining about being subtracted from all the frolicking cousins and the delicious food. Any other time, I would've felt privileged to be nominated by him on his adventures, but my enthusiasm was clouded by the aroma of food and gossip at home. Of course there was no denying him and so I joined the hunt grudgingly. Soon I came to know the reason for this honour. I was just a replacement for one of the uncles who deliberately remained absent citing a sudden stomachache! My mother fell back to her original cursing spells when she came to know that her plans for the evening would be interrupted and her lovingly prepared food would have to wait. My father, like most Indian men those days, wouldn't listen to his wife and set foot for his tiger trail anyway. On a normal day, mother would have packed some tiffin for our trip but today was not the day she would oblige. We had to come out empty handed and fetch for ourselves at dinner.

The forest air was cool and crisp, it was almost dark when we reached the fringe of the forest, but the moon was in it's full circle and it radiantly shone upon the landscape. The beauty of a full moon night in a dark forest is something I would fail to describe in words, for it's not a sight, rather an emotion to be experienced. Somewhat angry with my mother, father decided to cook a tastier meal for dinner right there in the forest, trying to compensate especially for me, the delicious meal that I had to give up on. So it was done, a number of forest hares were shot down by Rama with his slingshot. Rama's hunting skills in the dark were unmatched to any, he didn't even need a gun. His night vision was as good as any nocturnal animals'. Being a highway robber in the past, he had trained himself to be like a nocturnal creature. A tasty meal was made in a makeshift oven and relished. Father pronounced himself to be a better cook than my mother and I did not have the courage to object and nodded silently.

From his last experience with hunting tigers, father decided to camp near the watering hole and not inside the forest for the tiger to come. Now, this part of the forest was a little different than described in the previous story. This was the forest of Bhubaneshwar, around the area where now sits the city of Nayapalli. Bhubaneshwar, as we see it today, was definitely not what we had seen as youngsters. Even in our wildest dreams could we not predict that such thick forests and canopy of greenery would give way to such a crowded and buzzing city. Coming back to the forest, the stream where the tiger was predicted to come for a drink and the edge of the forest was separated by a large stretch of red barren earth which looked like a red desert. The distance between the forest line and the stream was almost half a kilometer. My father thus ruled out the option of putting up a 'machan' on the trees to aim at the tiger. He was sure he could not get a clear shot or a good angle from so far away. A trench was therefore cut on the soil at a spot where the earth was soft and damp. The trench would just about fit the three of us snugly. It was covered with twigs and dry leaves from the top so that it didn't look suspicious to the tiger or other animals. It was quite uncomfortable, frustrating, damp and cold in the tiny trench to wait for endless hours, but that was the best chance we had. It was like lying in our graves waiting to be rescued by the tiger itself. We decided to take turns in keeping awake and had completely covered the trench from the top like a green and brown blanket. Only a small opening was kept in one corner to keep vigil on "the" tiger or any other tiger that may come for a drink. By the time we settled down in the trench and covered up ourselves it must have been midnight. It was an unforgettable experience, there were so many unfamiliar sounds that came right from the watering hole, from ahead of us, behind us and from above us that I didn't know whether to feel heroic or to panic and quit. To be honest, there were moments I wanted to flee from all of it and go straight home to bed. But there we were, waiting patiently for the man-eater, and even a non-man-eater wouldn't go unhurt that night, looking at Rama's enthusiasm. Although, we didn't know how to tell a man-eater apart from it's polite cousins, for they all look the same!

Forest mosquitoes are stupid! First they sing and dance around you in a trance-like frenzy and then they settle down on your flesh with so much of an announcement, that all you do is rub them to death with your palms and "'swish"! mosquito massacre! City mosquitoes, I realised later in life, are smart, they trick you and suck your hard earned blood without your permission, much like some corrupt politicians do. In about half an hour, the three of us that night had wiped off generations of mosquitoes, but I can swear they were huge. Our mosquito killing spree was interrupted now and then by peculiar noises from the watering hole and the forest. We took breaks and strained our ears to look for "the" noise we were waiting for. Some deers came and drank and left, followed by a red fox and some hyenas, but no tigers on our menu. It was over two hours then and I was completely agitated by the song and dance show of mosquitoes, I wanted to sleep. My restlessness was a sign of my being an amateur, while the more seasoned hunters that were dwelling with me showed extreme composure and patience.

Another hour passed by without much drama and then we heard a sound that made us jump in our seats! The noise came from the forest side, it was a wild wild sound, something like the crashing of trees and thunderous bolts, the sound of rustling of dry leaves, followed by some madness. It seemed like someone was trying to bring the whole forest down! We then heard the trumpet, fierce and sharp, declaring its presence proudly and with warning. Yes, it was a wild elephant who seemed to be very agitated. We feared the worst as the sound approached closer to our trench. Suddenly, everything became calm, Rama peeked out to look for signs of danger.

Elephants are usually gentle and sensitive, the wild elephants like to mind their own business and are happy if humans mind their own too. But on certain occasions, especially during the breeding season, some male elephants may become savage, chasing other animals out of their way and damaging crops and trees. Some entered villages or farms and created havoc, people used all methods to chase them out. In cases where they repeatedly caused chaos or harmed someone, they were declared "rogue" by the local authorities. There was a ban and a fine was levied for killing elephants, on the other hand, a prize was declared for taming or terminating rogue elephants. Remember, things were not the same a century back, neither were the emotions surrounding animals. When I see the youth swelling with emotions for animals today, I feel a sense of guilt and disgust for what we have done in the past. Somehow, when we were in the middle of an action, we never realised the threat we were bringing upon the coming generations. For us, it was the opposite feeling, of the pride of protecting men from the wild, maybe, that was the need of the hour. The tables have turned and we need the wild to be protected from men today.

From the way the elephant rampaged through the forest, we feared it was one of the notorious ones. Few weeks ago, there was news of a single tusker creating havoc in some nearby villages, urging the local 'Raja' to declare it "rogue". However, there was no news of it's sightings for quite some time and we were now almost sure that this was the same one. Rama, straining his eyes in the moonlit night, peered through the trench and saw an enormous elephant standing still at the edge of the forest, sometimes swaying its head furiously. "Maybe it will come to the stream for a drink". My father was immediately alert and more so on hearing of the rogue elephant's rampage some weeks back. He asked Rama to check if the elephant had one tusk or two. The problem was that this particular one was moving alone. Elephants that move in a herd, with females and calves are usually safe but a furious single tusker, moving alone, in the mating season was something to be dreaded.

Rama confirmed it was a single tusker, taking our collective distress a notch higher. We were in two minds again. If we wanted to get up from the trench and run away, there would be too much commotion and the elephant would surely charge us, rogue or not. In such a scenario, there would be nowhere to hide, because it can bring down any tree that you may choose to climb or chase you faster than your legs could carry you. Additionally, there were too many of us to go unnoticed. On the other hand, if we remained where we were and the elephant came towards the stream, there were high chances that it would follow a neat route to the trench and fall in it, turning us into ketchup! Our hearts were racing, a decision had to be taken fast. We were definitely not there to hunt elephants nor did we know if this particular one was the same elephant that was declared 'rogue'. Killing any other elephant would've landed us in severe trouble from the authorities. We looked at each other in the dark and decided to crawl out of the trench by making the least possible amount of noise and run for cover. My father instructed us to crawl on all fours on the ground so that the elephant may mistake us for some other nocturnal animals and let us pass. Rama started to remove the coverings from the top. On the very first attempt, he tried to remove a leafy branch used as cover, it slipped in his nervousness and fell with a swishing crash in our trench, bringing down two or three more branches with it on our head, making me squeal. The swishing of the elephant stopped and it looked in our direction, straight unto our trench. We froze in terror knowing what would come next. If the five thousand pounds of fury decided to charge in our direction, we would need no Hindu rituals to cremate us thereafter, for all of us would be buried in the trench for eternity.

The elephant started moving cautiously towards the trench as if to inspect the source of the noise of the crashing and screeching. There was no time to waste or to observe anymore, as it inched closer, my father picked up his .500 Bore Rifle and aimed. He had to be quick and accurate, for if the bullet missed the mark and hit it other than the head, it would run amok, there was no telling in which direction it would run. The moonlit night seemed a blessing for we could easily see the elephant closing in. Father aimed for the head but just in the nick of time, the elephant moved sideways and the bullet hit it somewhere in the ribs, or so we guessed. Afraid of a full sweep charge, father shot a second round, and that too, missed the head and lodged itself near the chest. The beast gave a piteous cry and with loud trumpeting sounds it ran through the forest. We felt sorry and relieved at the same time. The noise it raised from pain would've melted even the sternest of hearts but we were not left with any option that night and couldn't blame father for his decision. No one wanted to go after the tiger that night anymore and we left for home as soon as it was deemed safe. Back home we decided not to speak about the elephant we injured, for a sense of guilt lingered within all of us for a long time. Usually, the younger siblings would anxiously await our return and come with hungry ears for the tales of adventures we brought back from the forest. On this particular occasion however we didn't divulge anything lest we be in trouble for injuring an elephant.

Two days later news came in that a "rogue" elephant had died with bullets in it's chest six miles away from where we hit it. No one came to claim the prize!

SHIKARI BABU'S WIFE

My mother was an extremely sophisticated and well learned lady when she was not angry. She belonged to one of the most affluent Pandit families in Assam at that time and settled with her fortune of husband and children in Odisha's Cuttack district. She was a no-nonsense woman and a strong feminist all her life. I have never in the ninety years of my life seen a more fearless woman than her. Precisely, she was scared of 'nothing'! It was a Herculean task to manage a team of nine howling children, but she did it like an ace! All said, no one comes between her Betel leaves (locally called Paan) and her. It was like a domestic art those days, practiced by men and women alike. "Paan", as most Indians would be familiar with, is a refreshing stimulant made using betel leaves and areca nuts and a plethora of fillings, making people more psychotic through generations. She, like most women in Odisha those days, used to find solace in it, especially when father was away for a while, leaving the burden of managing the whole family on her.

Mother, when she came to my fathers house for the first time after her marriage, she almost cried! There was an air of secrecy in the house and the servants acted strange, restricting her movements around the house. Those days in India, marriages were mostly arranged, with the bride and groom getting a pleasant or unpleasant surprise on their first night after marriage, for that is when they were first allowed to meet! Trust, therefore, was built after matrimony and not before. Brides were selected on the basis of looks and dowry while the grooms were selected based on family reputation, wealth and his fitness, of course caste and religion were the biggest deciding factors. Many women were married on false promises and deceptive reputations and their lives were ruined forever, my mother was well aware of these at a young age and went cautious immediately. "What are they hiding"?

"Why are certain rooms locked from outside"?

"What are the strange noises coming from the locked rooms"?

"Why am I being barred from going near them"?

Then came the biggest shock, when she saw a manservant secretly washing feeding bottles in the pond. Were there children in the house whom she hadn't been introduced to?

"Is my husband already married?

Has more wives?

Is he a widower with children?

Has he remarried using falsities?"

My mother lost her mind and stopped talking to everyone in the house until my father told her the secret. When she was told the reason finally, she burst out laughing hysterically. The rooms below that were kept locked from outside had tiger cubs, bear cubs and other small animals that father used to bring back from the forest while going hunting. They were well cared for and fed by feeding bottles sometimes and made for fine gifts for the Royal families where my father was often invited.

The Young Princes and Princesses would constantly pester their parents to bring them tiger cubs or other infant animals to play with. My father was often requested to bring upon orphaned animal babies for the local Rajas who kept them as pets.

Father had strictly asked all the servants in his house to keep this a secret from his new bride, fearing she will judge him as a heartless man and not love him, or worse still, she will throw them away. Mother did neither, instead she started nursing the cubs like her own children and kept on persuading him not to separate such tiny babies from their mothers. Father eventually obliged, when he brought in his own brood of little humans who anyway took up all the space he could afford.

When my father started with the timber business, I was quite young, ten or eleven years maybe. During this phase we moved to Bhubaneswar for a few years. The timber was brought from the forest to the Bhubaneswar Railway Station by our trucks, which were then loaded in goods trains and sent to the then famous "West India Match Factory" in Dakshineshwar, West Bengal. It was therefore beneficial to stay near the railway station.

Having been an ex-employee in the Railways, father had many friends and colleagues from the Railways, staying in Odisha. One of them was a retired British national, Mr. Godwin. He had a decent-sized bungalow just across the Bhubaneswar Railway Station and had an even decent sized family. At my father's request, he agreed to rent out the front portion of the bunglow to us. The bungalow had an open verandah which led to the front garden. Both Mr. Godwin and my father loved gardening and it was evident by the spectrum of colours that smeared the garden all seasons. There was a small plantation on the right hand side of the bunglow that belonged to the Godwin's and yielded pulses. Skirting this plantation was light woods that merged further into forests. At that time, this was the only house in the whole station area. Bhubaneswar station today is nothing like what it was then, bordered by a canopy of green trees and forests. We stayed there for a few years and the memory of it is still fresh in my mind.

One day, when I was about fourteen years of age or so, my father wanted me to accompany him to Calcutta (now Kolkata) for some business meeting. It was decided that my younger brother Gidi, too, will accompany us on our trip. Travelling to another city was an exciting opportunity then, especially for youngsters like us. My mother was left behind to look after the rest of the family, along with our semi-coward helper Bhola and our old great dane "Baga". Baga was the love of our lives, he was named Baga for he resembled a tiger cub when he was young. Once a cuddly ball of energy, now reduced to a lazy old dog who would look for all sorts of funny excuses to get up on our beds and nap.

Our trip lasted for about five days and was full of new experiences and excitement. Me and my younger brother couldn't wait to get home to our siblings and discuss our trip over a cup of tea. When our jeep halted at the entrance of the house, a hasty Bhola came running to help with our bags. He fumbled something to my father in a sorrowful tune. His expression alarmed us and we knew instantly something was not right. In a matter of two minutes, my mother appeared at the gate with our youngest brother Poltu (as we lovingly called him) and both were crying. I clenched my fists, in anxiety, not knowing what bad news she was about to divulge. "Baga is no more"! she wept and all our eyes started stinging collectively, including my father's.

On the second day while we were away, it started to drizzle lightly in the evening and everyone had moved indoors, while Baga was forgotten outside. He himself didn't mind the rain and remained quiet, for he loved the garden as much as he loved our beds! He was tied with his chain to a sturdy Hibiscus tree whose shade kept him dry. After dusk, my mother realised that Baga was still outside and asked Bhola to fetch him indoors. Bhola went out to the garden with a kerosene lantern in hand to unchain Baga. From a distance, he could see Baga sitting upright below the tree but when he went closer, he had a strange feeling. Baga usually got up and woofed and wagged his tail when taken indoors but today he sat still as a stone. Bhola froze in terror when he realised what lay in front of him. The figure that sat upright was not Baga at all! It was a panther sitting on Baga's lifeless body. It apparently seemed to have killed the dog there itself and was either taking rest or guarding its prey. It didn't run away seeing the lantern or Bhola approaching, instead it snarled, warning poor Bhola to back off. Baga's dead body and the iridescent eyes of the panther was enough to scare Bhola out of his wits. He threw the lantern up in the air screaming, "tiger, tiger!" and ran indoors as fast as his legs could carry him.

Once within the safety of the house, Bhola described to my mother what he witnessed outside. My mother was an extremely strong lady, Baga was like her child. Instead of breaking down in sorrow, she got really furious and wanted vengeance immediately. She picked up my father's 12 Bore gun and aimed from the window that faced the garden. She shot two rounds in the direction of the hibiscus tree where the panther was last seen and hoped that one of the bullets would hit him or at least scare him away.

There was a loud bang and immediately the garden bore various muddling sounds. There was the sound of rustling of leaves and swishing noises filled the air, as if someone was writhing in pain and trying to move forward. My mother and Bhola were sure she had hit the panther. The noise stopped abruptly and my mother in her mind, painted a bloodied picture of the panther, lying dead, deservingly. She wanted Bhola to go out and check after sometime but Bhola fell at her feet seeking mercy for his life, swearing that if spared today, he will procure three generations of faithful servants for our family's service, being the progenitor himself! So, it was decided to inspect the scene only the next morning.

Finally, at the break of dawn, Bhola and Mr. Godwin went out to the garden where Baga lay. The dog's body made for a grisly sight but the panther's body was nowhere to be found. They continued to search for some clues, like bloodstains, etc. to arrive at some conclusion about the panther's destiny but there was absolutely none. The search was given up and it was concluded that my mother had probably injured the panther who had obviously ran away. Baga was given a quiet burial in the corner of the garden by all the people present in the house that time.

At noon, Mrs. Godwin went to the garden for a stroll as was her habit, to collect fresh vegetables for the day. Something caught her eyes and she screamed in excitement, which poured the rest of the dwellers into the garden, assuming the panther had been found. When asked the reason for her deafening yell, she simply pointed a finger towards the bush fence that was used as a makeshift boundary for the house. There, in the dense grass, lay a huge python, about eleven feet long, with a bullet sewn across its body!

Younger me, during hunting days.

SHIKARI BABU'S SONS

Like many other Indian families of our generation, our family too was elongated to eleven members which included nine clamorous siblings. I'm the eldest son of my family and also the most unfortunate one to witness helplessly, some of my younger siblings lose the battle of life. We were five brothers and four sisters, many of whom now rest in a better place. "Gidi", my younger brother, was the closest to my age and one of my best hunting companion's after my father. We had a healthy and wealthy family life until one day my father decided to try a .500 Bore rifle on himself. Failing business and rising tensions in the family was too much for him to handle and he set himself free from all his duties, leaving behind an inconsolable wife and nine clueless children.

In the last leg of our business, I was mostly in charge of things, especially after my father's journey to the unknown land. To cut down on expenses, I drove our trucks, helped in loading and unloading and even cooked for the staff sometimes. With nobody to guide me any further, I started doing things my own way. Spending more time in the forest meant more wild encounters, more wild experiences and more adventures every other day. I was a reckless but skilled hunter by now, I usually never went 'after' something until I was requested to. I never planned an attack, never was calculative, depending largely on instinct. By the age of nine I had taken a fancy to the forests and had often gone barefoot to hunt small games. By the time I was an adult, I considered myself quite experienced already. I knew the forests and woods nearby like the back of my hand and often explored new territories of the forests. My favourite hunting companions were 'Gidi' and my father's friend 'Kanchun Da' as I lovingly called him. ('Da' in Bengali refers to an elder brother) He was a swift and accurate hunter, Kanchun Da, my friend and guide in the forests. Although he was close to my father's age, he was extremely friendly and jocund, which was the opposite of my father. He made everything jovial and light-hearted, cracking a poor joke now and then to loosen us up. With him we didn't have to be on our guard or be "disciplined", as father would have liked. Father went by rules, Kanchun Da by whim, making us at ease around him. Gidi was just learning to hunt but had inherited my father's lethal aim, mostly hitting targets spot on, even between the eyes. Neither me nor father encouraged him to go hunting so early on for we knew that the forests could be really perilous and unforgiving (those days)! My other younger brothers were really too young to fancy the forests. The love for hunting was distributed in a descending order among my brothers for they were gentler and gentler. The youngest one, 'Poltu', as we lovingly called him, was our exact opposite. He had a tender heart, full of compassion and started to cry when he saw animals in pain. He would go any length to nurse them back to health. The sister's, of course, were not interested in any of our feats and to-date criticises us for our acts. Respecting their sentiments, we too, never showcased our skills to them, nor displayed any heroism or pride in our deeds.

In the forests, it was mostly Kanchun Da and me after my father retired from life. Gidi occasionally accompanied us. Then there was Kanu Biswal from Khalikot. He was to me what Rama was to father. He was a faithful servant employed by my father ages ago, when we were children. We never called him by his real name. He was lovingly called "Kala Pahar", meaning the 'Black Mountain', ascribing to his dark muscular body and buffalo-like strength, also attributing to a local legend of the same name! This man, in his mid forties, was the most affable and honest man around, ready to sacrifice his life for the people he loved, we too adored him wholeheartedly. He was one of my constant forest companions over the years and somewhere, I felt a sense of safety and comfort when he was around. We all believed he could move an elephant with his sinewy arms! Me, him and Kanchun Da had a lot of adventures over the years, some of which I shall narrate in the following chapters.

As for my hunting career, which lasted about twenty five years, I hunted anything from a tiger to jaguars, bears, hares, deers, sambars, wild boars and some birds like water fowls, wild fowls, ducks, etc. Some were for it's meat, some were requested and the man-eater encounters were almost always requested. All the hunting expeditions did not lead to adventures nor did an adventure end in hunting. However, there are certain blood curdling episodes that I have experienced, which I would like to share with my readers. My humble request to all my young readers would be that of not being judgemental towards my youth and curiosity.

Our times were very different and we were not aware of the outcomes of what we did. Neither did we predict the mass extinction of such a large number of species nor did we dream of such rapid urbanisation. Looking outside my window as I write today, when I see this clamorous city, devoid of greenery or animals, my heart pines to return to the bygone era which never will be. Having said that, positivity turns the world on its axis, it is never too late to act, to reform, to replenish what is lost, to regret and rebuild. I write with the hope that some hands will come up with a solution to the havoc we have created and save the future of our planet.

MUNCH MUNCH!

When I was about twenty years of age, I was spending a few weeks at my maternal uncle's house in Kodala (in Odisha) during some family functions. The villagers there were mostly dairymen, raising livestock for a living, their cattles were mostly cows and buffaloes. During the summers, the sun rays all converged unto this land and parched the land, making it gape in thirst. The grazing grounds were reduced to parched tufts of inedible grass, sometimes, quite barren. Arranging fodder for livestock daily, was quite a Herculean task for the dairymen. This compelled many of the cattle owners to take their livestock to the deep forests to feed them, making themselves and their cattle vulnerable to attacks from wild beasts. Young cowherds were often attacked by bears, bison, boars and tigers but they had to keep on returning to keep the cattles from dying of starvation.

One very hot morning, I was taking a nap under the cool shade of a Banyan tree, not far from my uncle's house. Suddenly there was a tremendous uproar and wailing of women was heard nearby. I reluctantly shook off my slumber and got up to see the matter at hand. I gathered that a young dairyman had just been killed by a tiger, while out in the forest with his cows. The tiger had attacked one of his cows and turned on him while he was trying to flee. Now, it is a well known fact that tigers almost always will chase anything that turns its back and tries to run away from it, for tigers love chasing! I cannot comment on the modern day tiger's habits but atleast, from my experience, they always loved to chase anything that moved!

Now, there lay this young man's child-widow, a puny girl, hardly thirteen years of age, bewailing her husband's death. She was rolling on the ground with dishevelled hair, filling the air with her disconsolate shrieks. Meanwhile the elderly women of the neighbourhood blamed her for bringing about her husband's end with her evil face (whatever that was supposed to mean). The victim's mother, unable to bear her sorrow, fell into some sort of trance, cursing the next three generations of tigers, while prancing around like a mad woman. Unable to bear the cacophony of blames that the women doused each other with, which clearly had nothing to do with the tigers' primal instincts, I excused myself from the scene.

In the afternoon, under the same kind Banyan tree where I was sleeping earlier, a meeting was called by the white haired men of the village to mourn the loss of the black haired victim. Also to try and trace the tiger and kill it before it starts its own killing spree. Someone from the nearby village informed me that this one was not a man-eater but often preyed upon cattles in the past few months. It never killed humans until this time. It was also informed that the said predator was a male Royal Bengal tiger.

A small group of semi-skilled hunters with semi-lethal weapons and semi-nourished physique volunteered to join the hunt and I invariably had to join them and take the lead. Being more experienced than them and also bearing a better rifle and muscles, the villagers readily agreed upon me taking the charge.

We went to the spot where the tiger had attacked them. I was astounded at how deep this man had penetrated into the forest to feed his cattles and couldn't find any suitable reason for him to go so far. It took us almost an hour by foot to reach the spot! It was in the thick of the forest that they were attacked. The place had almost no sunlight to touch the ground, darkened by dense foliage above and around. No wonder the lush spot attracted the cattle for a feast. There lay the cow, with its neck torn down and stomach half eaten out, it made for a severely gruesome vision. The dead man lay about thirty metres away from the cow. It was pre-decided that the body would not be claimed by his family, until the tiger was killed. Those days, many families did not even cremate the bodies eaten by tigers, neither did the tigers spare much to be cremated! The dead bodies of a kill were usually kept for a day or two and used as bait to lure the tiger, for tigers always return to their kill. In this case, maybe because the tiger was not a man-eater, it didn't touch the man's body at all. The dead man lay as if in a deep slumber, sleeping peacefully because all his worries were over and neither did we want to disturb his eternal sleep. There was only a deep cut on his neck, probably the same wound from which he died, we did not have the heart to inspect his body further and left it as it is.

After a brief discussion, we agreed upon a spot to make a 'machan' and keep watch for the night. A tall tree with strenuous branches made for the most comfortable resting space for the night. We had a light supper packed for us with love and hope by the villagers and took our positions as soon as it was dark. Darkness settles earlier in the forests than anywhere else and by six in the evening, you can hardly tell who is sitting next to you. I decided to make up for the nap that I earlier lost in the day and we decided to stay awake in shifts through the night. You don't quite get to "sleep" on a machan in a forest, the weird noises and insects would ensure you don't get sleep but you can always doze off in a semi-conscious sleep, the forests permit that much. In about three hours from then, I was nudged gently by one of the younger lads. There was some noise beneath. Something had approached the dead cow and made a snarling sound. We sat up alert at the sound ready with our torches and guns, waiting to aim. When you are hunting in the dark, with little or no visibility, your best friend is the torch. While one man holds the torchlight, the other aims and the light from the torch often temporarily blinds nocturnal creatures. A pack of hyenas had sniffed their way to the dead cow and rejoiced at the feast. We decided to scare them away, since the cow was our bait for the tiger. Nothing much happened thereafter as we once again settled comfortably on the machan trying to take a nap. Occasionally, we swayed our hands to hush away the nocturnal insects and mosquitoes trying to feast on us. After an hour had passed, we were alerted by a distinct sound of some wild animal feasting on meat. We then heard the repulsive sound of crushing bones! For sure the tiger had returned to feast on it's kill. It must be finishing off the half eaten cow, I presumed. My father religiously believed that one should not kill an animal while it is eating, for then he brings evil upon himself. However, I wanted to be sure that this was the tiger and nothing else, that was feasting below us. I switched on the torch and directed the beams to the cow, but this time I was even more surprised to see that sitting next to the cow was "nothing"!

We all were equally confused. What was happening? We were sure that the noise was made by a tiger or some big animal eating flesh. Then the realisation set upon us, was it feasting on the dead man instead? The sound of the crushing bones was that of a human! The tiger was out of sight and by no means we could aim at it. We didn't know about the presence of any man-eater in the forest and therefore did not expect the dead man to be the target. We had thus set up our machan facing the dead cow. There was no way we could tell if this was the same tiger that the victim's mother cursed or any other man-eater who came upon a sudden feast; in any case, it was a man-eater for sure. We had to climb down in absolute silence to get somewhat close to the spot where the tiger was feeding and got a partial view of the awful sight that made me nauseated in disgust. Under the given circumstances of a deadly dark night mingled with the spine chilling sound of crushing bones, it was enough to scare the young lads out of their wits. I wouldn't say I was feeling very valiant either, so it was mutually agreed that we would return to the machan and wait for the tiger or tigress, whatever it was, to finish it's meal and rest, for that's how tigers behave. We could then take our own sweet time to take position for the shot. No man, however good his night vision is, could equal the nocturnal instincts of the tiger and suppose the torchlight was to fail us, we would have been severely handicapped in the darkness. It was almost four thirty in the morning and was about to dawn, so we decided to take advantage of the time and wait for another half an hour or so till there was some light at dawn. In about fifteen minutes or so, the tiger seemed to be satiated with his or her meal, for the chomping and the crushing sound ceased to bother the forest. As the sound stopped, we waited for some time to gather all our courage and climb down again, walking as cautiously as possible. We assumed that the tiger may have left for a drink or left the leftover for a later meal but when we closed in to about thirty yards or so, we could partially see the tiger's form in the dark, as huge as it can be, lounging carelessly next to the dead man, whatever was left of the poor thing. It licked and cleaned it's paws just like a domestic housecat. When I looked closely at it, I realised it was a very large male cub, man-eaters were usually more old and experienced than it. Tigers take to human killings mostly at old age when they are not agile and fast enough to chase a four legged prey. Humans are an easy target. Some turn man-eaters very young, if their mother's were man-eaters and fed them with human flesh as cubs. Some take up the trade when crippled, especially by porcupine quills, etc. However, this one looked very young to be a voracious man-eater. Why he decided to go after the human when there was a juicy cow lying next to it amused me. Not expecting to find it in such a close range, I signalled the younger boys to climb to safety but keep holding an angle since too many impatient hunters would make chaos and spoil our chances. There is always a chance of missing the mark or deflection of bullets that may lead to a non-substantial injury to the tiger, which may then in all its fury, launch a counter attack. No one should ever come in the way of an injured tiger.

Once the lads were safely perched on branches, I went a half circle round the tiger and took cover behind the stump of a dead tree. That day, since we were well prepared, I was carrying my father's .500 bore rifle and one of the other hunters had a muzzle gun aimed, just in case! The first shot from my rifle went piercing through the air and hit it somewhere near the shoulder. The tiger did not understand what hit him so suddenly and jumped three feet off the ground like a startled cat. When it fell on the ground, it came upside down. My second shot was not well aimed and fired in a hurry since I was bitterly scared it would come charging upto me. The second bullet, however, struck it in the jaws and though not killing it instantly, made it outright crippled. It lay on the ground now, trying to make some sort of a growling sound but before I could assess the situation, a third bullet hit it in the head, killing it immediately. I had not pulled the trigger a third time and by the time I realised that it was one of the boys from the trees, who turned acutely impatient, they came hollering down the trees in heroic jubilation. I had to shut them up and give them a piece of my mind. I told them that I was disappointed and that aiming from so far could be extremely risky. First, that I didn't like any disturbances when I was hunting, second, the noise they made in rejoicing could wake up even the dead. There is an old saying that "You never know the tiger is really dead until you skin it". Of course, I forgave their passionate blood and warned them that the huge beast in front of them may still be alive. Their celebration stopped abruptly and this time even without me saying, they climbed the trees on their own. I looked at the brutal display that lay in front of me and was nauseated at the sight of the dead man's bowels eaten out. We both were killers there, one dead and one alive, it could've been any of us breathing that day. We both were predators but I was the one that had a better shot at life, aimed with modern ammunition and help at hand. It was a man-eater for sure but it still was a majestic tiger to be felled. I took a few deep breaths and sat down heavily on the stump of the dead tree where I had earlier taken cover. We waited for about fifteen minutes and then the boys perched down and found a long stick to poke the tiger to check if it was alive. It didn't move, so we inched closer and found it to be stone dead. The boys again started screaming and cursing, this time with even more intensity. I made up my mind that day to rather go hunting alone and face the perils than go with Ostrich brained boys.

The sun was up and bright by then though not much of it reached the ground. It was decided that I would go back to the village alone and inform the people about our doings. They would then go and fetch the carcass of the tiger and cremate the dead man's remains in the forest itself. The young boys remained to protect the dead from all sorts of claims and vouched to return only after the dead man's cremation.

When I reached the village and broke the news, the victim's mother fell at my feet, much to my discomfort. She said something about revenge that I couldn't understand clearly amidst her sobbing and choking but I deliberated that she was thankful. I waited for sometime, while the villagers geared up for their duty in the forest, I was given some tea and biscuits meanwhile. I then came back to my uncle's place with a tired body and mixed emotions. The next morning, the villagers came to my uncle's house and brought the tiger's skin to me as a way of saying thanks. This was not my first tiger encounter but definitely one that was really memorable.

ROYAL BENGAL ON THE PROWL

In Hindol, Odisha, once there was news of a tiger prowling at night in the villages, picking up cows, goats and whatever it could lay its paws on! Every villager would be terrified to stir outside at night and occasionally had even heard the tiger growling in the vicinity of their cottages. Even lovers abstained from their rendezvous in the dark!

In all Indian villages, even now, it is a common habit to relieve oneself in the open fields or atleast away from home. Thanks to modernisation or Westernisation, whatever you call it, this habit is decreasing at a healthy rate. Back then, the Indian house was a ceremonious place, a temple in itself, therefore believed to be extremely sacred by it's dwellers. Any thought of causing impurities inside the house was a strict "no-no", especially from the womenfolk. Most of the villagers had to run to the fields, even at night, when nature growled in their stomach. The more affluent families would build a toilet a little far from the perimeter of the house. In any case, it was like surrendering oneself to the evil forces of nature, especially at night, making oneself vulnerable to threats from men and beasts alike.

This particular tiger was not known to be a man-eater, however, the very thought of coming face to face with a hungry tiger was enough to keep the folks indoors at night, even when they were in bad need to relieve themselves. The situation became unbearable as days passed. More and more reports of missing cattles poured in and ultimately the villagers came home for help. When father was alive, every little problem with wild animals in the nearby villages used to be reported to him first, especially those of tigers. Father was 'their' endeared "Shikari babu", their trusted man. Sometimes, even the Tehsildar or the Magistrate used to come home to tea and discuss excitedly about tracking down some wild animal creating ruckus; mostly, jaguars and bears. With my father now gone, I was yet to earn the trust of the villagers which they had willingly bestowed on him. However, being his eldest son and by now an experienced man in the forests, they attached some credibility to my abilities. I was no Jim Corbett, nor was I any expert with tiger trails but somehow, I found my own way of doing things and often ended the trails successfully. Not every trail that I chased ended in success and not every success entailed severe planning.

Being a localite myself, I knew many of the villagers by their funny names, ranging from Nonda, Gonda, Honda to Joga, Khoga, Boga and was fairly accustomed to their even funnier ways of conducting life. When the news of a prowling tiger was brought in, I was expected to search this "devil" or 'Sola Bagho', (local slang) and terminate it so that they can return to the fields and do their job without worrying about the tiger watching their private moments!

Most tigers have their areas ear-marked, their hunting grounds, which may stretch for miles. They even abandon old hunting grounds and move on to new areas for the fear of being too predictable. Like humans; experience, youth, size and speed plays an important role even in the tigers' lives. Young, full grown cubs, usually assist their mothers in their hunts, while an amateur tiger may go starving for days while sharpening their hunting skills. The older they grow, the wiser they become, for instance, once a tiger has learnt his lesson from chasing a porcupine, he would never repeat the mistake in his life, no matter how hungry he is. With age, comes more skill than speed and they polish their techniques with every new kill. It was a burden to trail this particular tiger and bring it down, for it also became a master in 'hide n seek'!

The next evening, we formed a team; me, Kala Pahar and Gidi, my younger brother. Other than us, there were also some small groups of hunters from nearby villages who were working individually or in groups to track the tiger down. The next three days were spent in trying to locate the tiger's whereabouts. It would suddenly appear in one of the nearby villages, pick up a goat or a calf and vanish into thin air. This was one of the most difficult chases of my life that had completely exhausted and bored me out over the course of three days. We walked, walked and walked through forests, camped at neighbouring villages and resumed our trail but this clever thing left no clue behind to follow. On the fourth day, I was so tired and agitated that I thought of giving up the search altogether. It was my younger brother's positive attitude that propelled my legs to move on. After a hearty lunch on the fourth day, we were back in the forest where we got our first clue, thirty miles from where we started our trail. A half eaten cow lay in thick bushes, well hidden from sight. We discovered fresh blood stains on some leaves and even some recent pugmarks. We decided to camp nearby. It wasn't a long wait this time, for the monkeys in the nearby trees started screeching strangely, which was an alert for an approaching tiger. Me and Kala Pahar were not new to these monkey-signals and we thus moved to safety. In a matter of time we saw the elegant lady, striped regally, she came about and started sniffing the prey. This was one of the smartest tigresses I had witnessed, for sure she knew she was being watched. She sniffed around for sometime and quietly retraced her steps back to the thickets. I was perched on a leafy tree, it's leaves swayed and ruffled and obstructed my vision considerably. The tigress was moving out of sight, it was the ultimate test of patience for me. For the past four days we were combing the forest for her and now, when she was so close at hand, I was about to lose my chance and had to start all over again. This thought crossed my mind like a flash of lightning and the fear of losing my chance made me shoot at the retreating tigress. It was definitely not well aimed for I could hardly see her properly and I do not know where it hit her. I saw her falling to the ground and it tried to drag it's body by stretching the two forelimbs on the ground. Maybe the bullet had broken her hip bone or hit her back, making it difficult to move the hind legs. It writhed in agony and brought down the whole forest in piteous cries. All sorts of voices joined in, the birds screamed, the monkeys screamed and some other animals made screeching sounds in unison with the roars making it an unbearable cacophony of blames. The tigress kept grumbling in pain but managed to drag itself behind the bushes out of our sight, I could not shoot again and relieve it of all it's pain. I felt a strange guilt settle into my nerves. I went into a reverie where all the sounds raised by the fauna seemed to me like a thousand voices blaming me for injuring a poor animal in search of food, worse still that it didn't die and is in extreme anguish. My brother called out to me from another tree and I woke up as if from a dream. The wounded tigress could come back if it had any strength left and seek revenge, so we stayed on the trees for as long as we could hear her moan. For about an hour, we could hear her groaning but it also became more distant and feeble before it finally stopped. It would have been wrong to assume her dead, for I had only hit her back, injuring it not fatally and in all probabilities, it was taking cover nearby to check on it's wound. The dread of a wounded tigress kept us in our places for quite some time until I thought it was safe to set foot on ground. Kala Pahar advised it was best to leave for the night and come back with more people the next morning to check if it was still alive.

We climbed down the tree and very carefully, made our way out of the forest. We were far from home and too weary to go such a long way back that night, so we stayed in one of the nearby villages. That way it would've been easier to follow up on our hunt the next day. That night, I hardly slept, blaming myself for the half hearted aim, a job that could have been done better. I felt pity on the tigress as it was only trying to satiate it's basic needs, more so because I left it injured and in pain. Each hunt taught me a new lesson and I tried not to repeat my mistakes. I mentally calculated the distance and the angle that would have made for a better aim and thinking about the day I dozed off at dawn even with roosters screaming their lungs out to the sun. I was so tired that I refused to get up even for a delicious breakfast consisting of cow milk kheer and puris (local delicacy). After a lot of coaxing by Gidi, I finally stirred, freshened up and headed straight for business.

Although the villagers were terrified of the tigress and were very thankful to us for our hunting mission, yet, somehow, no one wanted to take ownership of the situation and act accordingly. They were cordial, polite and smiled from ear to ear but when I asked them for the following favour, everyone retreated from their enthusiasm. Now, to be honest, me, Kala Pahar and Gidi were all scared to enter the forest to continue our search for the injured tigress in fear of being avenged. I had a plan in mind, for which I needed assistance from the villagers. A tiger would never attack its prey from the front or so was commonly believed. Usually it takes the prey by surprise, by pouncing on it from the rear and for very large prey, from the sides. Taking advantage of this knowledge, I wanted to take two buffaloes with me into the forest and let them lead the way, while we cover up each other, armed, from behind. There were two benefits to this, first, that animals have a better sense of impending danger than we do and thus the buffaloes would be able to guide us better. Second, if the tigress decided to launch an attack, it would never come from the front fearing the lethal horns of a pair of hefty buffaloes and we would be well prepared for an attack from the rear. The best advantage would be that of numbers. The feline species takes calculated risks and an injured tigress, in this case would most certainly back off seeing the crowd. The problem arose when the villagers refused to lend us their buffaloes for this purpose. They feared that the injured tigress would first kill us and then kill their dear buffaloes and create a massacre in the forest and no amount of reasoning or cajoling could make them yield. After asking around the village and looking at glum faces, I finally had to place an assurance that if the buffaloes were even a bit injured, I would buy them off. To this, they readily agreed and handed me two well-behaved buffaloes to take along. However, I managed to plead with their owner to come along, just in case the buffaloes decided to rebel. Again, I had to assure his wife and mother that he would be back safe and sound and in case something happens to him while I come back alive, they will be compensated handsomely. To this, the wife also readily agreed!

After wasting two hours putting a price on the buffaloes and their owner, we finally headed for the forest. It was about mid morning then and the sun was in all its glory. The man feared so much for his life that we had to place him at the tail of the buffaloes and we placed ourselves behind him. We showed him the direction and he led the buffaloes towards the spot where we had last seen the tigress. Few metres from where the bones of the dead cow lay, the buffaloes came to a halt and started to snort and huff, behaving strangely and restlessly. Their owner nudged them to move on but they refused with human-like nods. Maybe they were scared at the sight of the eaten out cow or did they smell fresh blood? They simply didn't budge. We took it as a sign and waited vigilantly but nothing happened and it continued to happen nothing for over twenty minutes. Atlast, the owner, whom we jokingly named "Bhera" for he trembled like a scared sheep, became anxious and wanted to return home with his buffaloes. Since the buffaloes too expressed their desire to leave, we let him go. After parting ways, with no horned beasts to cover us now, we became extremely cautious, as if expecting a full blown attack. We came upon the place where I had shot the tigress and there sure were bloodstains on the grass and dried leaves. We could clearly see the ground disturbed where the tigress had tried to drag herself with her forelimbs. The trail further led us to a hideous thorny bush where Gidi's leg got injured and we gave up the trail to tend to him. He had a deep cut on the calf muscle when he forced to move himself through the thorny bush and we thought it was better not to loiter around with an injured man in the forest.

No more killings of poultry or cattles were reported for the next few days. We had come back and told the villagers that their "devil" was injured and maybe even dead but they still kept indoors at night, just in case. Several days later as I was preparing to go on a business trip to Calcutta, some villagers came to see me. I knew their faces well for refusing me their buffaloes but I greeted them warmly. I was told that their "devil" had been found dead near a stream, all eaten out by jungle crows, vultures or whatever but strangely, all it's claws were missing!

MAN-EATER ON RAILWAY TRACKS

It was a gloomy monsoon morning, with an overcast sky that promised to burst anytime. There had been enough rain to quench the earth in the past few days already. I was travelling from Cuttack by train and was heading to Hindol for some work. Accompanying me on my journey was a dear friend whom I respectfully called Ramen 'Da'(elder brother) for he was elder to me. Ramen Da was a city bred man with no inclination or fancy whatsoever for hunting and such sports. He was an amateur with forest treks and seldom accompanied us during hunts, although he was a frequent visitor to our home. The purpose of this trip was quite dull and had nothing to do with hunting so I wasn't carrying any guns or rifles that day. I only had some spare bullets in my sling bag, which I almost always carried, along with other not so lethal contents.

When we boarded the train from Athagarh, it was drizzling already and only assured to turn into a downpour. Me and Ramen Da, once seated comfortably, engaged in a conversation over a cup of hot tea served by the local hop-on-hop-off vendors, common in the Indian Railways even today. A rainy day, a hot cup of tea, a close friend and a train journey all combined, could make even a dead man smile. As we were discussing some hot political topic of the day, some Bengali passengers who overheard us poured in their comments, uninvited, all at once and in blaring voices. If a Bengali man on a political subject starts with "arre moshai"(oh Mr.), that's it, pack your bags and jump off the train or wherever you are for you will never win an argument over politics with a Bengal bred man. Neither will he let you escape without hearing his political forecast for the century! Safely take this advice from me for I'm Bengali too!

Our arguments and tantrums flew faster than the train and we were so immersed in our world of politics that we didn't notice what fields and what trees flew past the windows. On any other day, when there were no aggressive political discussions with aggressive Bengali passengers, I liked to sit back and relax. I liked to relish the enchanting nature and devour its thriving flora with my eyes. I often sat marveling at the scenery that the trains ran parallel to. This was not an unknown route to me, infact, I was quite often on the same train on the same seat. I had even marked out a favourite window seat for myself which I invariably occupied if it was not taken. On this particular day, however, I had completely forgotten about that seat and about adulating the flora of my homeland.

The compartment became tense and loud and seemed to perspire, with the rain beating the roof, trying to cool off the chaos inside. So immersed were we in arguments that we hardly noticed the train coming to a sudden halt in an unlikely place. I was quite familiar with the halts made by this particular train enroute to Hindol but this was not one of them. This however gave us more time to debate and consume a few extra cups of tea. Only after it was standing dead for too long to raise an alarm, did we break up the altercation and turned to the matter at hand. It was almost half an hour then that the train hadn't moved an inch and showed no inclination to move either. Some eager passengers had hopped off the train and went to enquire about the reason for the delay. It was drizzling slightly then and some men opened their umbrellas and walked away from our compartment towards the engine, to talk to the driver perhaps. Two young boys came running back looking scared and tucked themselves into a corner, urging us to shut the doors and windows of the compartment. They mumbled something about a tiger and I instantly knew I had to disembark and see what the matter was. By the time me and Ramen Da reached the engine, there was already a small crowd of men in grave looking faces, talking in whispers. There was also our locomotive driver and a GRPI (Govt. Railway Police Inspector), who looked quite worried. When we joined the party, we came to know about an unfortunate incident.

Mr. Peters was the government appointed PWI (Permanent Way Inspector) on that route. He was a middle aged, Anglo-Indian man (as was the term commonly used then), who was also a trained shikari. He, being deputed in a forest covered area, was extra cautious and was always armed with a rifle to counter-attack any miscreants or wild animals. His duty was to get the railway track inspected and give a "clear" signal to the next approaching train if all was good. For this purpose, he had at his command, four to five trolley men, who would do the actual inspection of the tracks while he would supervise them. A trolley attached with wheels, of the same width as the tracks, was used to inspect the tracks. One or two men used to stand on the trolley and two men were to give it a good push from one end, upon which it would start rolling smoothly on the tracks just like the train. The trolley could travel quite a long distance, without a second push, for there being hardly any friction between the tracks and the wheels. It kept moving smoothly, allowing the people perched on it to look for any signs of danger or defect on the tracks, like a broken track, a fallen tree, etc. Also, any small animal scurrying on the tracks would be alerted by the trolley and they would run away unharmed. On this occasion, the trolley men had just come back from inspection and were still on the trolley, while Mr. Peters was settled cosily on his wooden armchair, puffing his tobacco pipe. On one side of the track, there was a small raised platform and an even smaller, dingy office room. We were told that it was his habit, out of respect for his dear life, to always hold on to his rifle with one hand, even when he occasionally dozed off, like many of our government employees still do!

This part of the land was a forest area, part of Ranibania, a small village belonging to the local "Raja". The railway track passed through the middle of quite a thick forest. Those days, there was a dense forest that stretched for miles between Atagarh and Hindol and tigers were not unknown in that area. From where we were standing, I could see that both the sides of the track had quite thick vegetation running parallel to it.

The trolley men were engaged in a conversation with Mr. Peters, seated in his chair, when suddenly they witnessed a tiger leaping out from the thickets and pouncing on him from behind, toppling poor Mr. Peters from his chair. They saw him struggling to get hold of his rifle and finally being dragged away by the beast. The trolley men got so scared at the sight of the tiger, which they knew to be a man-eater, that they left the trolley waiting on the tracks and ran for cover wherever they could. Each one of them had run to the nearest tree available, climbed up in haste and refused to get down until our train reached the spot. From the trees, they had heard Mr. Peters screaming out for help for a long time, so they assumed he was alive and conscious even when out of sight. They were all wearing long black raincoats due to the rain and informed us that even Mr. Peters was in his raincoat when he was attacked.

It had been a little over forty minutes from the attack I gathered and the tiger couldn't have gone too far carrying the weight of a full grown man. So there was a chance, however slim, that he was still alive and could be rescued. By then, the group had become large and noisy and everyone urged the trolley men to repeat the incident over and over for them, as if they had bought tickets to a circus, not the journey! When I asked around for volunteers, no one wanted to risk their life by attempting a rescue mission, that too in the rain. I was completely unarmed for the purpose but I was also the only experienced shikari in the group. I couldn't just wait there doing nothing. My inner voice told me something could be and had to be done. I vocally volunteered to go on a rescue mission and take my chances to see if the poor Mr. Peters could be saved. Ramen Da was definitely not happy with this decision of mine and was petrified with fear of being dragged along. He frowned angrily and admonished me not to show off or try being a hero and then pleaded with me to re-think, I winked at him to say "all is well"!

I asked the GRPI to arrange for a rifle if possible and that's when the trolley men suggested looking for Mr. Peters' rifle in the bushes. After searching for a while, we recovered his beloved double barrel rifle. Although it was in a lamentably archaic condition, yet that was the best we had at that moment and I was determined to make do with it. On further inspection, I found that the rifle had only one cartridge. Thankfully, I had some spare ammunition with me in the slingbag that I earlier mentioned. In any case, you hardly get to fire more than two rounds on the same man-eater, for either the tiger should be fatally injured with two or it will run away, in case it doesn't, you wouldn't survive to make a third attempt!

When I volunteered to go for the rescue, the crowd was jubilant, excited and cheered me to move on but a new problem arose. The GRPI refused to lend me Mr.Peters' rifle (a 0.12 bore double barrel rifle) and immediately took it in his custody. He doubted my ability and thought I merely hatched a plan to steal the poor rifle right under his nose. I had to open my sling bag and show him the spare ammunition to assure him that I was indeed a shikari. Even then, he said that it was his duty to keep the rifle in his custody until it was claimed by authorised people. I pleaded with him and tried to make him understand that we were wasting precious time in arguments, which could be put to better use by darting off to the trail. The crowd joined in, taking up my side and tried to cajole him further but he wouldn't budge. Standing in the crowd was an elderly man who was listening to our arguments with a grave face, he looked stern and had an aura about him. All this while he hadn't spoken a word, now, he came forward and introduced himself as one of the "Dewans" of the local Raja (King). Although this was the period of British colonisation in India, yet, to that time, the local law and order was still with the Rajas of the areas. Coming to my rescue, the "Dewan-saheb", as we respectfully called them, ordered the GRPI to hand me the rifle since a life was at stake. He was superior in social rank to the GRPI and thus after a little hesitation, the GRPI finally gave up his custody. The Dewan told me to meet him at the Raja's residence and return him the rifle after the mission was over, suppose its owner was dead.

Once the rifle was in my hand, I dashed into the direction pointed by the trolley men, not even looking back to thank the Dewan! I only waved with the back of my hand, signalling a reluctant Ramen Da to pick up the trail after me. We had put the trolley men on standby, instructing them that they should immediately come in our direction if they heard a gunshot from us. The trail was supposed to be easy, for the earth was soft with rain and the pugmarks should be easily visible and followed. It was still drizzling slightly as we moved through the bushes and trees and started entering into quite thick woods. We moved as rapidly as possible, knowing fully well that each minute was precious, also trying to make up for the time lost in arguments. But we were also cautious, not to make much noise, lest the tiger is nearby and hears us. The wet soil considerably reduced the noise made by our shoes. The damp leaves lying in the ground do not rustle as much and small twigs and branches that are strewn on the ground, become more resilient to snapping when the earth is moist. Somehow, I thought that we were in luck, for the following reason: near at hand was the Charbatia Air base and some Air Force planes were doing their routine dogfight rehearsals at that time, making thunderous sounds overhead. Being a localite, I was pretty used to these sounds and I was sure, even the tiger was used to it by now. This noise from above was a perfect camouflage for the sounds made by us while rushing through the jungle. Pugmarks were visible here and there and made it an easy trail to catch up on, much as I had predicted. After walking deep into the forest for about thirty minutes or more, we saw the beast!

It was a mid-sized tiger, male, it seemed to me from a distance. It had it's back towards us, which was a good thing and it was panting heavily. About forty feet away from its tail was the upturned body of the PSI, face buried to the ground, unmoving and the black raincoat looking like a shroud upon him. I presumed him dead, for there was no movement from him whatsoever. We were again at an odd angle from the tiger, facing its tail but this was the closest that we could get to it unnoticed. There was no way I could aim at the head and get it down in a single shot, it could only be hit at the back. If injured, it would definitely take out it's anger on the poor PSI and eliminate the chances of his survival, if there was any. There was no time to even wait for it to change it's posture, for if it turned, it would be to rip a piece off the poor man's body for a meal. At present, it looked tired from the gruelling job of carrying a full grown man through the forest to its safe spot. I had to aim fast, before it decided to start its meal.

I aimed the 0.12 Bore, double barrel rifle towards its shoulder and prayed the almighty for all the luck He could bestow upon man in a split second, then pulled the trigger. "Click", the trigger went but no bullet escaped its barrels! I cursed the rifle, which was in a more pitiable condition than its owner. There was no escape, for the tiger had heard it alright, it turned its head and saw us! It snarled, putting its lethal teeth on exhibition and got ready to pounce on us. I had not prepared myself for this misfortune and there was no back up plan either. The tiger growled furiously and for the first time in several years I realised that coming face to face with a wild animal, even with arms, is not child's play. The way an angry tiger looks into your eyes, can paralyse your limbs and make a statue out of you. I was not even thinking anymore, working on instinct, I pulled the trigger of the rifle again, to fire a second round, although I forgot to aim it well. This time the rifle and the Almighty, both showed extreme mercy and a miracle happened! Both the bullets got fired simultaneously, trying to make up for the empty "click" sound earlier. I do not know what followed or where it hit the tiger or whether it didn't but the tiger sprang out of our way, aborted the attack and fled. For a few seconds, the green canopy started spinning around my eyes and it took quite some time for Ramen Da and me to believe we were still alive. When we were awoken from our spell, Ramen Da pointed out the broken tiger jaw and blood ahead of us. Most likely, both the bullets hit the tiger together, breaking apart it's lower jaw but not killing it immediately.

We climbed up the branches of a nearby tree and waited for sometime, just in case it returned. By then, the gunshot had alerted the trolley men and others waiting on the spot. They were requested to rush to the forest for help with some ropes, sticks, etc. Within half an hour or so, a small group of men rushed in hollering. They made loud noises intentionally to scare away any wild animals or tigers out of the way. Finally, we were in a position to inspect Mr. Peters' condition. When we turned him over, fearing the worst, he was found unconscious, with a deep cut in his forehead. We assumed it was by hitting some object on the way when being dragged by the tiger, that he fell unconscious. Other than a bite near the shoulder, he was not severely affected. The heavy rubber-like raincoat had spared his flesh from the tiger's tooth and nail. Near the shoulder, the raincoat was torn away by the tiger's teeth.

We brought him back all the way to the Inspection house and then revived him using a very old trick. A black pepper is put on a pin and burnt using fire, then held near the nose of the unconscious person. The pungent and hot fume is known to revive the person. Once he was conscious, he was sent to the Dhenkanal General Hospital where he was revived under more competent hands. About fifteen days later, he invited me to his bungalow for dinner and gave me his poor gun, both as a sign of gratitude and as a memorabilia of an adventure that we both will never forget.

Gidi(with rifle), during our timber business days

NO GUN? HAVE FUN!

There was a time when my father was a flourishing wood merchant, supplying timber for industrial purposes to many factories, within and outside Odisha. There was a small hillock near Hindol, which was locally called "Banka Mundi", (crooked head) owing to its crooked formation. Our labourers used to go atop the hill to chop down trees. The hillock had a dense green cover, dotted with Sal, Rubberwood and Sheesham trees, which were in high demand then. Our men would go to the hill, early in the morning and chop wood till about noon and leave for the day. These men were usually inexperienced daily wage earners, not really trained lumberjacks. Due to a lot of unemployment those days, many villagers would come seeking a job and were added to the list on a daily basis. Some of the experienced staff used to go along to guide them and give instructions on how to go about the job. Once the cutting was done, two or three of our accountants, including our very own Kanu Biswal (Kala Pahar), would go uphill to count the number of trees felled, count the logs, number them with black paint and make note of payments to be made to the daily wagers. Once all the notes were taken, the logs would be rolled downhill and collected below to be loaded onto our trucks and taken away.

One such morning, when two of our staff didn't show up for work, I decided to accompany Kala Pahar to the hills and help him with his chores. It was about 11 AM in the morning and the wood-cutters were almost about to finish their job. It was a bright sunny day with a pleasant breeze brushing our hair, as we cycled towards the hill. We had a favourite spot to park our bicycle, under a tree. Right next to our parking spot, much to our surprise, we saw a medium sized Royal Bengal Tiger, nonchalantly basking in the sun! It was a very unusual place for a tiger to be found, for generally they avoid paths taken by humans frequently and neither do they like to seek attention! It was hardly fifty yards away from us. When we got down from the bicycle, it turned it's head to take notice but didn't budge. The fact that it didn't take cover, seeing two full grown men approaching was also unusual. However, it seemed in no mood to disturb it's poise. We assumed it was just being a lazy cat! We were just two leaps away from it, was it in the mood to attack. It just looked straight into my eyes for a few moments, as if trying to read my intentions and asking me to back off and sat unperturbed. There was no news of any man-eater in that province at that time. We therefore assumed that we wouldn't resemble a delectable lunch to him!

We stood still for sometime, unable to decide what to do. Kala Pahar whispered that we should walk backwards, keeping our face towards the tiger, for it wouldn't attack from the front, if it wished to. It wouldn't have been advisable to run and we both knew that. We took very small and light steps and traced our way back, making sure not to make any sudden movements which may threaten the tiger. Being a bright sunny morning on a day to work, I was not expecting any wild encounters and neither was in the mood for a game and thus was completely unarmed. Kala Pahar used to carry a Burmese Baton at all times, which was a popular favourite among the people of Ganjam District in Odisha. It was a handy weapon that was usually carried by men to counter wild animal attacks or to fight off miscreants. It had a wide front and tapered towards the end and was about three feet in length. Kala Pahar had got it custom made and was severely proud of his possession. When struck with force, it could kill a man and critically injure even wild animals. However, it was no match to a rifle in hand, especially with a Royal Bengal Tiger trying to hypnotize you with its gaze!

With adventures and experience by then, I was quite composed with a lazy tiger or any resting wild animal in front. As long as they aren't preparing for an attack or agitated, they usually mind their own business. As long as tigers weren't declared man-eaters, they didn't unnerve me so much. Tigers and other beasts of the forest were a part of my daily life then. We often had casual sightings and were habituated to their presence around us.

In my sling bag was a bundle of papers supported by a thin tin foil, on which the papers were clipped onto for support while writing. It was an archaic version of modern clipboards. I had procured it myself, using an old Kerosene tin. It was dull on one side and shiny, like a mirror on the flipside. We recycled almost everything in our times and never even perceived a day of 'use-and-throw' would land on earth. Some mischief came upon me when we were about eighty yards away from the tiger. I slowly opened my sling bag that crossed over my body and took out the foil, devoid of papers. Using it like a proxy mirror, I showed it to the sun and guided the reflected beams unto the tigers' eyes, waiting to see its reaction. Kala Pahar chuckled at my prank and held on tightly to his baton, ready for the blow if required. One shout from us would alert our people uphill who would then hurry down making a lot of noise to scare away the beast. Assuming this, we thought we were in a safe spot and continued with our mischief like school lads. The poor cat was quite agitated with the harsh beam glistening in its face and tried to change angles quite a few times. It looked very perplexed, unable to fathom why the beams chased it from various angles and refused to leave it alone. It growled slowly and at last got up, looked over its shoulder and ambled into the jungle with a gait more sophisticated than a king's. Me and Kanu chuckled notoriously and continued our trek uphill.

FOOLISH FERVOR FAILS

After my father's demise, I had become quite occupied and absorbed in trying to keep the timber business alive. Initially, I tried to find out means and methods to stop incurring losses in the already failing business, which was challenging. For quite a few months I didn't have the time or leisure to go hunting and that bored Kanchun Da. He didn't want me to miss all the fun that we had together and often coaxed me to accompany him on his trails. I had no choice but to politely refuse him. When I refused him almost a zillion times, he was irked and promptly stopped talking to me. Meanwhile he befriended other shikaris to fill up the void created by my wilful absence.

When we finally repaired the bond, he brought home an over-enthusiastic, garrulous friend, who happened to be an amateur hunter. This person boasted of ridiculous feats that were impossible to achieve, like killing three tigers with two bullets and so on! Of course, I didn't laugh on his face and tried to be as polite as being a host would permit. Being a wealthy man's only son, Sukumar was what we call a "spoilt brat", who had the whim and fancy for the most unbecoming things. He would hardly take a 'no' for an answer and imposed his whims with such coercion that poor Kanchun Da had to almost always oblige. On the very first night that he stayed with us, he expressed his desire to go hunting for big games in the forest! I explained to him as politely as I could, that it was the mating season and the local authorities had barred all hunting expeditions for the time being. The rules would be relaxed only for a rogue animal or man-eaters. Of course, all my advice was futile. Sukumar hardly cared and rather persisted that no one will ever know who goes into the forest at night, besides, killing one or two animals won't ruin the whole biodiversity! On Kanchun Da's constant pleading, I gave in to this otherwise impossible and risky demand. The same night, Sukumar proudly displayed his expensive "Greener" gun to us, a valuable possession for any gun lover. Using high sounding words, he swore to put it to good use, at the very next opportunity.

The following night, after everyone else had fallen asleep, we set out in a small group of five men to gratify Sukumar's baleful desire. In the pitch dark forest, we used head-light torches to guide us. The torches, when flashed around, reflect the iridescent eyes of most nocturnal animals, making it easier to hunt. In about two hours from when we set out, Kanchun Da hunted a deer. This triggered both disappointment and excitement in Sukumar, who couldn't wait to aim his new gun at some unfortunate game. Two of our helpers who had accompanied us, were carrying the dead deer and were soon tired of loitering in the dark. They urged us to call it a night but Sukumar wouldn't relent. He pleaded with us to stay till his gun was inaugurated.

To keep his request, we roamed about some more in the dark. The darkness of the forest was so radical that night that it seemed to be a living entity, stretching its arms out to engulf everything in its way. It made the council of fireflies here and there seem like the only hope from being devoured by the blackness.

Towards the end of the forest, right where the village starts, Sukumar saw something in the dark and squealed in excitement. His head-light torch had reflected the iridescent eyes of some animal. Even before we could understand what was happening, he aimed and fired at those eyes! There was no growling or howling of any wild beast but some heavy animal was heard falling with a thud on the ground. In absolute euphoria, Sukumar screamed, "one down, one more to go" and aimed again! The two helpers who were following not far behind came running, screeching "don't don't don't" in an alarmed voice. Their dismayed voices made all of us freeze in consternation. One of them simply grabbed Sukumar's hand and snatched away his gun, much to Sukumar's disbelief. "Why did you aim there Sahib "? asked one of them in a hushed voice. "You fool", replied Sukumar quite agitated, "I can clearly see the burning eyes of a tiger, they always glow in the dark, give my gun back, there are more, I have to rescue all of you before they attack". What the helpers said next made the darkness spin thrice round our eyes. "Saheb, those are buffaloes tied at the edge of the forest and there are dairymen who sleep there too"! We were petrified with terror. Sukumar had shot a buffalo in all probability and could have accidentally killed humans! Thankfully he was stopped from aiming again and creating a mass grave there. To all this frantic discussion, Sukumar just pulled a poker face and replied, "Let's flee, no one is here, no one will know"!

We, of course, fled, but we knew it was all not so simple. Sukumar was a guest and nobody knew him but what about me? All the villagers nearby knew about my passion for hunting and that I was the only person in that area to possess guns and rifles, so naturally all fingers would point at me. There would be no escape from this and so once back home, we made a small plan to assess the situation ourselves.

Me, Kanchun Da and one of our helpers dressed as plain villagers, covered our faces and went to meet the dairymen on the pretext of buying milk. It was about 3.30AM then, almost time for the buffaloes to be milked, for buffaloes are always milked at dawn. We took some milk pans with us and went straight up to the dairymen. They were all gathered around a charpoy and were talking busily, discussing the gunshot nearby. When we approached them, the conversation that ensued was as follows:

Kanchun Da- "Can we buy some milk? Are the buffaloes milked yet"?

Dairymen- "No no, not today, go away, all the milk is pre-booked by our Sahab for his son's rice eating ceremony. We are not selling today"

Kanchun Da (trying to buy time as I threw torchlight around to inspect the scene) - " We really need milk, we will give you extra money, no one will know if you give a little bit milk"

Dairymen- "No, Sahab will be very angry if he comes to know, please go away".

Meanwhile, I kept flashing my torchlight at intervals to the tethered cattle to look for any signs of injury. One buffalo was sitting down and moving it's head viciously, which caught my eyes and I guided my torchlight to it. The poor creature was bleeding profusely from its nose. It looked like it was unable to groan but was trying it's best to stand up, in vain. I signalled Kanchun Da to close the conversation and we returned home.

By about 7AM in the morning, the owner of the cattle came home to meet me. He was a rotund, rich and influential man, who owned about a hundred buffaloes in that area. He seemed calm, he only said, " I know, your men killed one of my buffaloes, it was hit in the mouth and died an hour back, what now"? His calmness seemed more threatening than his cursing would be. He spoke slowly, leaving some space for us intentionally, as if to let us justify ourselves. Those days, a full grown buffalo would cost anywhere between Rs200 to Rs250. A few days back I had purchased a buffalo drawn cart for Rs400, so I was aware of it. Without much hesitation, I owned up and apologized to him. Irresponsible hunting could lead to hefty fines and even jail and we were quite aware of that. We accepted our fault easily, for any contest would have only worsened the situation. Sukumar himself came out and owned up, much to our surprise. We settled the matter by paying him a compensation of Rs 220. This was the year of 1952 and that amount was a fortune. He left us with a subtle warning, to be more careful in the future and we were forced to express our guilt for the fiftieth time that morning. Once he got the money, he left silently, not before inviting us for his son's rice ceremony!

WHY I LEFT HUNTING

We were hunters, guilty of claiming innocent lives. Hunting in our times was a sport, passion of many and a challenging way to kill time. Many would have had their ego hurt when a friend refused their offer to go hunting. In trying to sharpen our skills and boost friendship ties, many lives of precious animals have been lost over years.

In the more passionate years of my hunting career, I was often invited to go on hunting trips as a companion or guide. We went for leisure, to entertain guests, to fulfill requests for meat and sometimes to get rid of rogue animals. Going out in the forest with a friend or two to catch a game was a popular thing those days which brought havoc in the forests. I do not intend to sugar-coat my erstwhile intentions to force respect out of my readers, rather I want to unfold the truth that led to the grim situation of the wildlife that we see today.

My early life was spent in Cuttack, Odisha. I grew up alongside the beauty of the majestic river "Mahanadi" and its picturesque banks. I often took leisurely strolls with my friends or family members by it's banks or it's expansive 'barrage' to soak in the cool breeze and refreshing scenery. The water of the river used to be clear blue and tempting in the winters and summers while it became muddy brown and ferocious during monsoons. The blue water merged seamlessly with the backdrop of the blue tinted mountains that formed a chain on the other bank of the river. The healing sound of water rushing through the barrage used to lighten up my dampened mood whenever I visited it. At a younger age, the blue mountains on the other side used to entice me and carry me into a reverie. I never had the opportunity or requisite to visit these hills or it's foothills, covered with a thick layer of verdant forest, teeming with wildlife. I only got to visit them in the year of 1960, during the last phase of my hunting career.

I had a dear friend 'Mongu', who was a middle aged Gujrati businessman, grown quite affluent over time. He had a farm house on the foothills, near the bank of the 'Mahanadi' river. His farmhouse had a big orchard around it, he also owned a few acres of paddy fields surrounding his property. Mongu once invited me to his farmhouse from where we were to explore the forests nearby. Although not a hunter himself, he proudly possessed a single barrel rifle, which he occasionally used to scare away the monkeys rampaging his orchard. He mostly scared them away by firing blank shots! He would often bring guests to his den and entertain them by taking them to hunting trips in the nearby forest. The forest, as such, started at the other side of a shallow stream that crossed his house, about three hundred metres away. It stretched for about two kilometers to the foot of the hills like a thick green blanket aiming to wrap the hill. The hills too, were veiled with tall trees and bushes, making it an ideal shelter for wild animals.

I readily accepted his invitation, excited that my childhood fancy was turning into reality. The next morning, we crossed the mammoth river by a 'Launch'(ferry boat) and travelled another six kilometers on foot to reach his farmhouse by noon. Mongu had engaged two caretakers and a cook for his farmhouse and to look after his property. They ran errands, looked after his guests and pampered him whenever he visited. One of the helpers, who looked too old to me to be ordered around, came up to me in the afternoon and proudly showcased his country made muzzle gun which he owned. He declared that he used it to scare away any wild animals that invaded the property and for safety at night. During the paddy harvesting season, due to some reason, many wild animals had to be reprimanded for trespassing the property! Mongu also had a pet dog, a German Shepherd, who would guard the farmhouse and the adjoining areas. When we went in, we were welcomed by the helpers and the dog with equal enthusiasm! The helpers hurried to prepare tea and food while the dog licked Mongu's face with much satisfaction. Like most Gujrati's, Mongu was a strict vegetarian but ordered a delicious meal of mutton and rice for his not so compassionate companion! After dinner, we set out on foot to explore the nearby forest and were joined by three more men. They came in as enthusiastic guides and bearers, in case we had a game to carry back home. These men were from the adjacent village and worked as forest guides and helpers for a nominal fee.

If a particular method makes you successful numerous times, you tend to get superstitious about it. We Indians are vulnerable to superstitions and I am not completely free from its grip either. I believed that being in odd numbers or carrying an odd number of cartridges would bring good luck in the forest, ward off any evil and bring success in the trails. That day, although we were five men, carrying an odd number of guns and cartridges, yet all my superstitions fell flat and futile. Even after walking in the dark for about two to three kilometers and flashing our headlight torches all the way, we came across nothing, except for some owls and rabbits. We didn't shoot any small games that night, lest the sound of guns scare away the big games. At about 2 AM, we returned back, frustrated and empty handed. Mongu and the guides were pretty sure that the forest was blooming with big games and were quite despondent at not being able to stand up to my expectations. Mongu especially didn't take it well and was somewhat embarrassed at fuelling my imagination all evening.

Although not a shikari himself, he set out early the next morning, along with another guide whom he had summoned. He was determined to bring me back something from the forest to cheer me up and to keep his word. Since it was very late at night that we went to sleep, I naturally went into deep slumber and had no knowledge of my friend's intentions.

We were to reach the jetty the same morning by 11AM to be on time for the 'Launch' to take us back. I had planned to wake up by 8AM and then get ready to start. However, at around 7AM, I was awakened by a familiar whistling sound coming from the direction of the orchard. "It must be a Sambar" I thought! Sambar's are large deers with antlers native to Odisha and other parts of India. My shikari instinct made me jump off my bed and head straight for the gun. I rubbed my sleepy eyes and was confused to find the barrel gun missing from its place, replaced by the muzzle loading gun instead. That's when one of the helper's hurried in to inform me that Mongu had decided to turn shikari for the day, for my sake and had gone to the forest with his priced barrel gun. The other helper came running in followed by the cook and all of them were extremely excited to give me the news of a Sambar sauntering in the orchard. They urged me to hunt it for them for its meat, by whatever means available. The cook handed me the muzzle loading gun and cheered me on.

I took the gun and went out. The Sambar looked to be a young male deer with beautiful antlers crowning it's head. If I shot it down, it was large enough to call the whole neighbourhood for a feast. When I attempted to lock the hammer of the gun, I realised it was already locked. I cursed Mongu for leaving with the better weapon that he hardly knew how to aim! I later realised that it was a defective gun, with the hammer not fully locked, because the trigger could be pulled with a little bit of maneuvering. It took quite some time for me to understand how the gun functions and I finally locked it in position. By then the Sambar sensed some impending danger and jumped over the fence belonging to the neighbour and unaware, landed in a tank of cow dung intended for manure. Due to it's heavy weight and slender legs, it got stuck in the tank, unable to move an inch.

When I turned towards it to aim, something else caught my attention. From a distance I could hear a distinct howling sound made by a pack of wild dogs. I was not new to this sound. These were nomadic wild dogs, usually in large packs, ferocious, lethal and hungry. They were locally called 'Bolia'. Wherever they went, they spread terror among other animals, hunting down even the mightiest of the lot. Due to their presence, most wild animals, including tigers, fled from those areas. Now it all started making sense to me, as to why the otherwise fecund forest turned barren, stripped of it's thriving wildlife. They were the reason why we didn't find any wild animals in the forest the night before. Naturally, the animals must have fled to safer zones, fearing the ferocious fangs of the wild pack.

I realised that this Sambar too was chased by the dogs from the forest. Running for life, it entered the village in the foothills, knowing well perhaps that the dogs never entered the village. They usually will give up the chase on the perimeter of the village or around human presence, for humans are the biggest predators! The whole experience changed for me and I felt sorry for the trapped deer who had come to the village seeking shelter. It had come to the humans with the hope of being rescued from the dogs and now it lay stuck in the pit, immobile. I walked up close to the fence and when I looked carefully, I saw it's pitiable eyes, large and innocent, it looked towards me as if begging for mercy; asking in silence for help. This beautiful creature with those scared and timid eyes, full of pathos, shook me up completely. We usually shot at deers from a distance, but this time I was face to face with it, feeling its breath, its nervousness, its fear. A sense of guilt descended on me like fog on a winter morning.

In front of me was an innocent life, unaware of human character, it entrusted its safety on us, seeking protection from the villagers. On the other side was me, proud, slipshod and greedy, a gun in hand, ready to shoot it down mercilessly. But this time, I couldn't bring myself to pull the trigger looking at it's pleading eyes.

By then, a group of men had gathered around me, cheering me heartily to shoot at once, the target being easy for a fancy evening banquet. I lied to them that the trigger was jammed and was suddenly not working. Moreover, killing it in such a situation would be unethical and 'unsportsman-like'. I requested the group to help it out instead, hoping that they too would feel the pangs of sympathy for the deer that I was experiencing. I asked them all to lend a hand to the poor deer and hastily excused myself from the scene, fearing they would ask for the gun for further inspection. Their cheering stopped abruptly and they mostly looked crestfallen, half annoyed with me. Someone even called the owner of the gun "useless".

From the garden, where I came back to, I could clearly see a deadly scene unfolding before me. The villagers started talking loudly and excitedly. They began to call out instructions to one another and in a matter of a few minutes they came back in a larger group carrying whatever they could find to kill the trapped animal. I saw large stones, axes, batons, sticks and my heart sank as I feared the worst. Mongu wasn't back yet and the helper and cook who stayed behind, didn't dare to join the hooligans seeing that I was already cursing them from afar. Although, I discerned they were equally disappointed with me.

I stood there petrified, as horrified as the Sambar, while a gruesome scene was laid out before us. I made one last desperate attempt to halt them and called out to the group to stop but my request was overshadowed by their sinister enthusiasm. They pounced on the frightened deer and lynched it to death in the most pathetic and merciless way one could imagine. Being a shikari, I wasn't unaccustomed to the sight of blood, pain or death but even I closed my eyes at this macabre bloodsport. To be honest, something in me wanted to protect the deer that day. It would be a lie to say that the thought of gunning down all the men attacking it didn't cross my mind. A permanent disgust took birth in me at that moment. I could feel the pain of the Sambar very closely and decided to give up hunting animals from that day itself. I was shown the mirror by the Almighty and took it as a sign from above. When I went hunting, I never got the opportunity to look at the scene objectively. Now, realising what a cruel and unforgiving race we humans were, I decided to permanently withdraw my contributions to it.

The poor deer abandoned its home, the forest, being chased by the wild dogs and came to the village in hope of being rescued. Knowing little that it entrusted it's life to the most selfish and cruel species on earth. Not only did they hack down a trapped animal brutally but also shamelessly rejoiced like war heroes. I vowed to kill no more animals, not even to save the humans from rogue animals.

I agree that the realisation came over me after much harm was done but I'm thankful it washed over me at last. The earth is meant to be a shared home for men and beasts alike. We have no right to decide on their fate. There is indeed no heroism in killing a defenseless animal. As if by divine intervention, new laws were soon implemented to protect the wildlife. Many Rajas and even the Government in some places banned hunting altogether. It was good news for the forest, the wildlife, there was a new hope to revive and replenish what is lost. Just when I thought the menace was finally getting over, a new era of poachers began!

www.ingramcontent.com/pod-product-compliance
Ingram Content Group UK Ltd.
Pitfield, Milton Keynes, MK11 3LW, UK
UKHW021647190726
13853UKWH00001B/107

9 789354 278457